THE MIGHTY SANTA FE

William H. Hooks ✦ *illustrated by Angela Trotta Thomas*

Macmillan Publishing Company   New York   Maxwell Macmillan Canada   Toronto
Maxwell Macmillan International   New York   Oxford   Singapore   Sydney

The author and artist wish to thank John Pagliaccio, toy train aficionado, for his contribution to the depiction of Granny Blue.

The publisher wishes to thank Lionel for permission to use the Lionel name and to illustrate Lionel trains.

Library of Congress Cataloging-in-Publication Data
Hooks, William H. The mighty Santa Fe / William H. Hooks ; illustrated by Angela Trotta Thomas. — 1st ed.   p.   cm.
Summary: At Christmastime, William has to leave behind his cherished train set when his family goes to visit William's frightening great-grandmother. ISBN 0-02-744432-5 [1. Great-grandmothers—Fiction. 2. Railroads—Trains—Fiction. 3. Christmas—Fiction.] I. Thomas, Angela Trotta, ill. II. Title. PZ7.H7664Mi 1993   [E]—dc20   92-17026

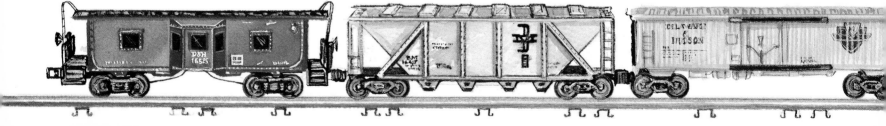

For William Robert Davies
—W.H.H.

For my husband, Bob, with love;
special thanks to the Sadorfs,
Sarah and Bobby
—A.T.T.

William sat scrunched in the corner on the back seat of the van. Stuffed all around him were packages wrapped in bright paper with ribbon bows. In his pointed green cap, he looked like an unhappy elf from Santa's workshop.

Thunk! William kicked the back of the middle seat, where his sister, Molly, sat next to Matt, the new baby.

Matt woke up with a cry.

Mom twisted around from the front seat to quiet Matt.

Molly twisted around and swatted William.

"Stop that!" ordered Mom.

"William kicked us," said Molly.

"What's the matter with you, William?" asked Mom.

"I wanted to bring my trains," mumbled William.

"Okay, Dad," said Mom, "it's your turn to explain."

"Number one," said Dad, "there was no room in the van for your train set. And number two, there won't be room enough at Granny Blue's house to set it up."

"Remember, there'll be nine grown-ups and ten children to play with at your Great-Granny Blue's," said Mom.

"They're mostly girls," said William.

"Oh, goody, goody," squealed Molly.

"You do have a boy cousin," said Mom.

"He's a baby," grunted William. "Are we about there?"

"We've got another hour," said Dad. "I hope we make it before the snow starts to fall."

"I just saw a snowflake," said William. "I hope it snows right up to the top of our van."

Within a few minutes, Dad had to get the windshield wipers going. And half an hour later, it was snowing really hard. William rubbed circles on the foggy windows to see outside.

It was almost nightfall when the van pulled into Granny Blue's driveway. Several uncles and aunts burst out of the front door and slogged through the snow to the van. They all talked at once:

"You had us some worried!"

"I could just imagine you all snowbound on the highway!"

"This van is stuffed like a Christmas stocking!"

"Here, let us help you get unloaded."

William, Molly, and Matt the baby were swept into Granny Blue's wide hallway in a flurry of snowflakes mixed with uncles, aunts, and cousins.

"Come on back to the kitchen," called Aunt Sara. "Granny Blue's been in a tizzy waiting for you to get here."

William hung back.

"Come on, William," urged Mom. "Granny Blue's waiting."

"I'll stay with the packages," said William.

"Granny Blue wants to hug you," said Dad.

"I'm scared of Granny Blue," whispered William.

"Come on," said Dad, taking William by the hand. "Granny Blue won't bite you on Christmas Eve."

Granny Blue sat close by the fire in a big rocking chair. To William she looked like a shriveled-up little person. She was too wrinkled and old to be a child. But she was not much bigger than one.

"William first," cried Granny Blue.

William stood still.

"Is something the matter with you?" asked Granny Blue.

Dad nudged William a little closer to Granny Blue. Quick as a trap, her arms snapped around William. She hugged him close.

William squirmed. Then he pulled back.

"William is a little put out," said Mom. "We couldn't bring his train set."

"A child should always have a train set," said Granny Blue, looking at William through squinty eyes.

William turned away from her stare, but he liked the way her eyes twinkled.

Suddenly the lights went out.

"What happened?" someone yelled from the hall.

"Must have blown a fuse," said Dad.

"It's not the fuses," answered Granny Blue. "Power lines must be down from all this snow."

William glanced up at Granny Blue. The light from the flickering fire made her face look scary. She laughed and bobbed her head up and down. "Now we can have a real Christmas," she said, cackling. "An old-timey one like when I was a mere willow switch of a girl."

Aunt Sara called the power company. "You say the lines are down? Well, when can we expect to have them fixed?"

There was a pause.

"Well, thank you," said Aunt Sara.

She hung up the phone. "No power tonight, and maybe not even tomorrow for Christmas day. I'll fetch some candles. Some of you men better start a fire in the parlor. We've got a blizzard on our hands."

The last bit of daylight disappeared as Granny Blue's house began to glow softly with candlelights and roaring fires in the parlor and kitchen. The children crowded around the big fireplace, roasting marshmallows, while the grown-ups helped Aunt Sara get dinner on the table. Granny Blue kept an eye on the marshmallow-roasting pack of great-grandchildren.

"Watch it there, J. T., you're starting to smoke!"

"Not so close to the fire, Willie Mae!"

"Look out, Molly! Yours is on fire. Blow on it, child!"

For a while William forgot about his trains.

"Sara!" called Granny Blue. "I think the children should have a picnic."

"But there's a blizzard outside," said Aunt Sara.

"Who's talking about outside?" asked Granny Blue. "I mean a winter picnic like we had when I was a willow switch of a girl. You just spread my lone pine tree quilt on the floor before the parlor fire and let the children have their supper picnic-style. And for dessert they can have fresh snow mixed with cream and brown sugar."

Granny Blue turned back to the marshmallow pack. "How would my great-grands like a winter picnic?"

"Yay! Yay! Yay!" roared the children. Even William managed a good, strong "Yay!"

After the winter picnic, most of the grown-ups crowded into the parlor. Dad played Granny Blue's pump organ and everyone picked a favorite Christmas carol. When they were all sung out and the younger cousins were falling asleep, Granny Blue said, "Time for 'Silent Night.' And sing it softly while you take the little sleeping ones off to bed."

The bedroom was cold, but William felt snug under the mountain of quilts Mom piled on him. Matt, Molly, and Mom and Dad fell asleep right away. But William couldn't sleep. He always played with his trains before going to bed. And he always made up a secret story about them.

He tried to make up a story by imagining his trains. It didn't work. He needed to feel the engine and touch the cars. He needed to run his fingers along the bumpy tracks and to rearrange all the miniature pieces that made up the station and the town and the countryside the train passed through.

He slept fitfully and woke again. Through the crack at the bottom of the door he could see a dim light coming from the hall. The door silently opened and Granny Blue, holding a flashlight, crept into the room as quiet as a snowflake.

William sat up. Granny Blue motioned for him to come with her.

William pulled the pile of quilts over his head. He listened hard, hoping to hear Granny Blue leave the room. It was so quiet, the only thing he could hear was his heart thumping.

He sneaked a look. Granny Blue was right beside his bed. She motioned for William again. He slipped out of bed and followed her out of the room, dragging a quilt behind him.

As soon as the door was closed, Granny Blue whispered, "Put that quilt around your shoulders. It's a magic cape."

William found his voice and asked, "What kind of magic cape?"

"Depends on where you want to go," answered Granny Blue. "And I think I can guess where you would like to go."

William shivered in the cold hall, then pulled the quilt around his shoulders.

"It's up there," said Granny Blue. She pointed with her flashlight to the narrow steps leading to the attic.

Granny Blue started up the stairs. She climbed slowly, resting a little on each step.

William wanted to rush back to the bedroom, but something seemed to be pulling him toward the attic.

Granny Blue disappeared inside the attic. It was suddenly dark on the stairs. William hurried through the doorway.

There was Granny Blue, almost lost in a jumble of boxes, trunks, and old furniture. She moved over to a large table that was covered with a dusty white sheet. "That's it," she whispered. "Come close, William. It's right here, right under this sheet."

William edged through the clutter and stood next to Granny Blue. She put her arm around his shoulders. Then she chanted:

"Blemeney, blimeney, blue!
Ah-chooka, chooka-choo!
Bite your thumb.
Spit in the dust.
Cross your eyes,
Close them tight.
Feel your body,
Growing light."

William squeezed his eyes shut. He thought he heard Granny Blue spit. She went on:

"Blemeney, Blimeney, blue!
Ah-chooka, chooka-choo!
Through wind and rain,
And sun and snow,
To many a place,
Wild and wondrous,
We two will go."

Granny Blue shook William. "Watch!" she hissed. She snatched the corner of the sheet and flipped it into the air, making a cloud of dust.

But was it dust? No! It was snow! Snow was gently falling on an old-fashioned village. And right in the center of the village stood a trim little railroad station. Soft yellow light glowed in the windows.

"Listen," whispered Granny Blue. "Do you hear it?"

"A train horn!" said William. "I hear it!"

Through the snow, with its headlight beaming, a train pulled into the station.

"What kind of train is it?" asked William.

"Blemeney blue! It's a Lionel® train—the mighty Santa Fe. And she's hauling a long line of passenger cars. Hop on, William! We're off for a snowy ride!"

The mighty Santa Fe chugged through the town, gathered speed as it passed a patch of snow-laden trees, and raced out onto the endless white prairie.

On and on the mighty Santa Fe slid over the shiny rails, snaking its way up the side of a gigantic mountain. Rain slashed down in silvery streaks, playing a rat-a-tat-tat on the roof.

Out of the mountains and into the desert streaked the train, chasing the blazing sun across an ocean of burning sand.

From the desert, the mighty Santa Fe charged through a vast sea of gently waving wheat fields.

Suddenly the sky turned a sickly gray. The wheat twisted and turned and danced wildly this way and that as a great dark funnel roared toward the Santa Fe. The tornado lifted the train from the tracks and sent it sailing like a feather through the air.

"Ah-choo! Ah-choo!" Granny Blue sneezed. "I knew that dust would get me. Sorry I knocked over the table. I bet we woke the whole house," she said as she scrambled to her feet.

They listened for a few moments, but the house was still and silent. Then they eased down the stairs and back to William's room.

As he stepped inside, Granny Blue whispered, "Through wind and rain, and sun and snow…"

William didn't hear the rest of it. He barely made it into his bed before falling asleep.

Christmas morning dawned like a frosty wonderland. The storm was over, the sun was out, and the snow sparkled like magic dust. There was still no power, but Granny Blue's fireplaces crackled and warmed the house.

The aunts, uncles, and cousins crowded around Granny Blue's Christmas tree, which was almost lost in a mound of presents. It took quite some time to sort out all the gifts. It took even longer to open the boxes.

All the while, William was groggy with sleep. And his head was heavy with dreams about a train ride. Dreams? He wished there were some way he could ask Granny Blue about the attic and the ride.

Finally the tree was clear. Granny Blue's parlor was knee-deep in boxes, wrapping paper, ribbons, and bows.

"Let's leave this disaster," Aunt Sara said, "and go in for breakfast."

The uncles, aunts, and cousins flocked into the kitchen. William held back. So did Granny Blue.

When they were alone, Granny Blue hobbled over to the little tree and lifted up the green flannel cloth that skirted it. There stood the mighty Santa Fe engine with a red bow tied around it.

"They missed one," she said, handing William the engine. "It belonged to your dad. He thinks all his trains were lost when your grandmother's house burned down years ago. But I saved the mighty Santa Fe. And now it's yours."

The table in the attic flashed through William's head—the village with the station, and all the passenger cars.

"Wasn't there a whole—"

Granny Blue pressed her fingers to his lips. "Sh-sh-sh! Just remember, there are wondrous places to go."

William hugged her. Then, as they walked arm in arm toward the kitchen, they said together, "Through wind and rain, and sun and snow…"